Compilation and cover art copyright © 2020 by Berenstain Enterprises, Inc.

All rights reserved. Published in the United States by Random House Children's Books, a division of Penguin Random House LLC, 1745 Broadway, New York, NY 10019, and in Canada by Penguin Random House Canada Limited, Toronto. The stories in this collection were originally published separately in the United States by Random House Children's Books as the following:

The Berenstain Bears and the Week at Grandma's copyright © 1986 by Berenstain Enterprises, Inc.
The Berenstain Bears and the Homework Hassle copyright © 1997 by Berenstain Enterprises, Inc.

Random House and the colophon are registered trademarks of Penguin Random House LLC.

Visit us on the Web!
rhcbooks.com
BerenstainBears.com

Educators and librarians, for a variety of teaching tools, visit us at RHTeachersLibrarians.com

ISBN 978-0-593-17609-2
Library of Congress Control Number: 2019951243

MANUFACTURED IN CHINA

10 9 8 7 6 5 4 3 2

The Berenstain Bears®

GRANDPARENTS Are GREAT!

Stan & Jan Berenstain

Random House 🏠 New York

The Berenstain Bears
and the
WEEK AT GRANDMA'S

When mama and papa bears
go away,
Cubs visit their grandparents
for their first long stay.

Once in a while the Bear family, who lived in the big tree house down a sunny dirt road deep in Bear Country, got out the family snapshots and looked at them.

"What are these?" asked Sister Bear, picking up a book of photos. "I don't think I've ever seen these before."

There were pictures of bears playing
tennis, canoeing, dancing, and having
all sorts of fun. The bears looked
like Mama and Papa, only they were
younger and thinner.

"They're pictures of Papa and me on our honeymoon," said Mama with a smile.

"At Grizzly Mountain Lodge," said Papa. "We had a wonderful time!"

"What's a honeymoon?" asked Brother.

"A honeymoon is a special trip couples take when they get married," explained Mama. "Getting married is a very special happening, and celebrating it with a trip is an old custom."

"As a matter of fact," said Papa, "we've decided to go on a *second* honeymoon. We're going back to the same place to play tennis, go canoeing, and have fun!"

"It'll be lovely," said Mama.

"A second honeymoon sounds like a pretty good idea to me," said Brother.

"Me too," said Sister. They scooted out of the room and were back in a jiffy with their vacation things.

"Oh, you won't be coming," said Papa. "Honeymoons, even second honeymoons, are just for grown-ups, not for cubs."

"But ... but what's going to happen to us?" asked Sister.

"It just so happens," said Mama, "that Gran has been after me to let you spend a week with her and Gramps. And this will be the perfect opportunity."

"A whole week?" said Brother.

"But we've never stayed with anybody that long!" said Sister.

"Well," said Papa, taking a few practice swings with his tennis racket, "there's got to be a first time for everything."

"What will we do for a whole week?" asked the cubs. "Where will we sleep? What will we eat?"

"Goodness!" said Mama. "Such a fuss about a simple thing like spending a week at Grandma's."

It didn't seem like a simple thing to the cubs. They loved Gramps and Gran very much, but...well, they just weren't Mama and Papa.

Besides, Gramps and Gran were sort of...*old*.

"What are you taking with you?" Sister asked Brother when it was time to pack. "I'm taking two books, my jacks, and my teddy, of course."

"These," he said, holding up some books and his best yo-yo.

Papa put their suitcases in the car trunk last so that when they got to Gran's, unloading was as easy as one-two-three.

Then, after lots of big bear hugs and kisses, the happy second honeymooners were on their way.

"It certainly is good to see young folks having fun," said Gran as she waved good-bye.

"*We're* the young folks," muttered the cubs. "*We're* the ones who are supposed to have fun."

"I'm sure you're hungry after your ride," said Gran when they went in. "How about some of my special honey-nut cookies and milk?"

"No thanks, Gran," said Sister. "I'm not hungry right now."

"Hey, these are really good," said Brother.

Sister sneaked a taste. They *were* good, but ... well, they just weren't Mama's.

"Now let's get you up to your room so you can get settled," said Gramps.

The cubs reached for their bags, but before you could say "Grizzly Gramps," they were gathered up, bags and all, and carried up the steep stairs. Gramps certainly was strong for someone so . . . *old*.

The room at the top of the stairs
was very nice—very nice, indeed,
but . . . well, it just wasn't home.

"Gramps," said Sister, "where do you suppose Mama and Papa are right now?"

"Well," said Gramps, "I reckon they're still on the road, just pulling into sight of Grizzly Mountain Lodge."

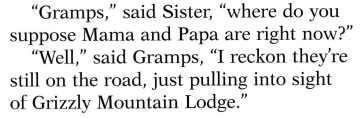

After they unpacked their things, Gramps thought the cubs might like to explore around the house.

While it wasn't home, it *was* an interesting house. There was the attic crowded with all *sorts* of interesting things...

Gran's kitchen with its yummy tastes and smells...

and Gramps's den. Gramps knew
how to build a ship in a bottle.
When the cubs asked him how
it was done, he just smiled.

"What do you suppose Mama and Papa are doing now?" they asked then.

"I reckon they've gotten into their tennis clothes and are swatting the ball back and forth," he said.

Over the next few days Brother and Sister found lots to do. They helped Gran feed her bird friends— more kinds than they had ever seen in one place. And Gran knew all their names.

They helped Gramps cut and smooth twigs for a new ship in a bottle. It turned out that he built them *outside* the bottle and then slid them in. It was pretty tricky.

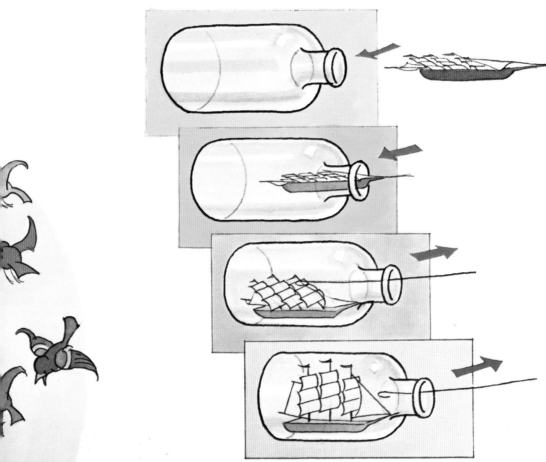

They went fishing in a special place Gramps knew about.

"Well," said Gramps as they returned with a fine catch, "I reckon that your mama and papa are out canoeing right now."

"I certainly hope they're having fun!" said Sister. "Because we sure are!"

"Hmm. Better get these chairs in,"
said Gramps after a fine fish fry.
"It's going to rain tomorrow."
    "How do you know?" asked Brother.
    "I can feel it in my bones,"
answered Gramps.

It turned out Gramps was right.

"Good," said Brother. "We'll be able to relax a little." Sister got out her jacks and he started to play with his yo-yo.

"Used to be pretty good with one of those myself," said Gramps.

Was he ever! Not only could Gramps make the yo-yo sleep and walk-the-dog, he could even do baby-in-the-cradle and round-the-world!

That evening, after a refreshing nap, they all went to Gramps and Gran's regular Friday night square dance.

Gramps and Gran didn't just watch. They do-si-doed with the best of them. They even won a prize—for Friskiest Couple.

"Goodness!" said Sister in the
morning. "This week really flew by!"

"And we learned so much," added
Brother, practicing baby-in-the-cradle.

"Gramps and Gran, how come you
know so much?" asked Sister. "So many
things! Why, you can even feel the
weather in your bones!"

"That's one of the good things about being an older person," said Gramps, smiling. "You learn something every day. So that by the time you're old enough to be a grandparent, you know quite a lot."

"Gee," said Sister, "I guess you and Gran are so old you must know *everything*!"

"Oh, no," said Gramps, laughing. "You never stop learning. Why, just this week we learned something very special. We learned how absolutely wonderful it is to be grandparents and have lovely grandcubs."

Then Gramps and Gran swept their grandcubs up in a big hug.

The next thing they knew, a familiar *beep! beep!* was heard. It was Papa tooting the horn. He and Mama were back from their second honeymoon and it was time for the cubs to go home.

After saying good-byes and
thank-yous, the Bear family piled
into the car and headed home.
No sooner were they on their
way than Brother and Sister
were bubbling over with the fun
and excitement of their week
at Grandma's.

"Well," said Papa, "sounds like you had a pretty good time."

"Oh, we *did*!" said Sister. "Papa, sometime you might want to go on a *third* honeymoon. Then we could spend another week at Grandma's."

"A *third* honeymoon?" said Papa. "I don't think anyone's ever gone on a *third* honeymoon."

"Well," said Sister, "there has to be a first time for everything!"

The Berenstain Bears
and the
HOMEWORK
HASSLE

If you're a bear for TV,
loud music, and fun,
how ya gonna get
your homework done?

Mama was sitting in her favorite chair straightening up her sewing basket when she sniffed the air and said, "What's that funny smell?"

Papa looked up from the evening paper and sampled the air. "Hmmm," he said. "I smell it, too. It smells like . . ."

"Garbage!" said Mama. "It smells like garbage."

Papa sniffed again. "Now, where do you suppose . . ."

"I'll tell you where I suppose!" said Mama, who had put aside her sewing basket and sniffed around the room. "It's coming from Brother's backpack."

And sure enough,
it was. There was an
old banana peel, a
brown apple core,
and a moldy piece
of bread in Brother's
backpack.

But that wasn't all there was in Brother's backpack. Among the books and papers was a letter. It was old and wrinkled, and it was from his teacher. Mama read it.

Then she passed it to Papa. After Papa read it, he looked across the table at Brother, who was doing his homework.

At least, he was *supposed* to be doing his homework. And maybe he was. But it was hard to tell by looking at him. He had a card table set up in front of the television, which was showing his favorite program, *The Bear Stooges*. He was listening to his boom box and talking into a cell phone at the same time. There was a Game Bear and a bowl of popcorn on the TV. And, oh yes, there were some school books and a paper and pencil, too.

"Excuse me, young sir," said Papa. "Is this the Mars space station?"

"I'll get back to you, Fred," said Brother.

He put down the cell phone and turned off the boom box. "I'm not quite reading you, Dad."

"You're not reading much of anything, according to this letter from your teacher. You may as well have *been* on Mars for all the attention you've been paying to your homework lately," said Papa.

"Letter? What letter?" asked Brother.

"This old, wrinkled letter that Mama found in your backpack," said Papa. The letter may have been old and wrinkled, but its message was clear.

Dear Parent
I regret to report that Brother Bear has fallen too far behind in his homework. Please call me.
Yours truly
Teacher Bob

"In my backpack?" said Brother. "I thought my backpack was private."

"When something starts to smell like garbage," said Mama, "it isn't private anymore."

Sister Bear couldn't resist putting her two cents in. "I don't see how you expect Brother to keep up with his homework. He has so many more *interesting* things to do. There's soccer, basketball, video games, going around like a big shot, and *girls*."

Brother turned on Sister. "Why, you little . . . !"

"That will be quite enough, Sister," said Papa. "Why don't you go do your own homework?"

"It's all done," said Sister. "See?"

"You call those scribbles homework, you little twerp?" shouted Brother.

"Now," said Mama, "let's everyone calm down and try to figure out what the problem is."

"I'll tell you what the problem is! The problem is too much homework! Vocabulary homework! Arithmetic homework! Science homework! It's homework, homework, homework! Every subject! Every day till it's coming out of my ears!"

"Uh-huh," said Papa. "Tell me, son, what is your homework for today?"

"Adding and subtracting fractions and memorizing two stanzas of 'The Bear Stood on the Burning Deck.'"

"That really doesn't seem like too much homework to me, son," said Papa.

Brother slumped and stared at the Bear Stooges, who were busy hitting one another on the head.

"I'm not hearing any sort of explanation," said Papa. "I guess that's because tonight's homework isn't really the problem. The problem is that you haven't been handing in your homework on a daily basis. You haven't been taking care of business. You've been falling behind."

"Gee, what's going to happen?" asked Brother as the living room phone rang.

"It's the BRS," said Mama. "For you, Papa."

"Take their number and I'll call them back," said Papa.

"What's the BRS, Mama?" asked Sister.

"It's the Bears' Revenue Service," said Mama. "They collect taxes."

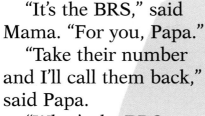

"What's going to happen," said Papa, "is that there's not going to be any more Mars space station. No more boom box. No more popcorn. It's just you and your homework until you're all caught up."

"But that'll take forever!" moaned Brother.
"Nevertheless," said Papa.

"You just don't understand!" said Brother, heading for the door.
"Where are you going?" asked Mama.

"I'm just going for a walk," said Brother.

As often happened when Brother had a problem and went for a walk, his feet led him to Gramps and Gran's, just down the road.

Gramps and Gran could tell Brother was in trouble as soon as they opened the door. After some milk and cookies, Brother told them the whole miserable story: the telltale letter, the missed assignments, the no television, the no video games, the no anything until he caught up. And he was so far behind that he'd never catch up.

"Oh, you'll catch up," said Gramps. "Your father did."

"Huh?" said Brother.

"Same thing happened with your dad when he was your age," said Gramps. "Of course, there was no television then."

No television, thought Brother. Wow! That would have been like *really* being on Mars!

"We had radio," continued Gramps. "We still have it, of course. But radio was like television then. It had great stories every evening. There was a Western called *Bearsmoke,* and *Buck Bruin in the Twenty-Fifth Century* was sort of like *Bear Trek* is now. And your dad listened to them while he did his homework. And he was big on sports, just as you are. So he fell further and further behind. I clamped down on him, just the way he's clamping down on you."

Gee, thought Brother. Papa *does* understand. The thought that he'd gone through it all himself made Brother feel a little bit better.

A stranger was meeting with Papa when Brother got home.

"He's from the BRS," said Sister. "It has something to do with taxes. It looks like Papa hasn't been taking care of business, either."

The stranger was about
to leave.
"We'll be glad to give
you a little more time.
But you're going to have
to catch up," he said as
he left.

And that's how it worked out. Brother
sat on one side of the card table, and Papa
sat on the other side.
It was a good lesson for both of them.

Gramps and Gran could tell Brother was in trouble as soon as they opened the door. After some milk and cookies, Brother told them the whole miserable story: the telltale letter, the missed assignments, the no television, the no video games, the no anything until he caught up. And he was so far behind that he'd never catch up.

"Oh, you'll catch up," said Gramps. "Your father did."

"Huh?" said Brother.

"Same thing happened with your dad when he was your age," said Gramps. "Of course, there was no television then."

No television, thought Brother. Wow! That would have been like *really* being on Mars!

"We had radio," continued Gramps. "We still have it, of course. But radio was like television then. It had great stories every evening. There was a Western called *Bearsmoke,* and *Buck Bruin in the Twenty-Fifth Century* was sort of like *Bear Trek* is now. And your dad listened to them while he did his homework. And he was big on sports, just as you are. So he fell further and further behind. I clamped down on him, just the way he's clamping down on you."

"I'm not hearing any sort of explanation," said Papa. "I guess that's because tonight's homework isn't really the problem. The problem is that you haven't been handing in your homework on a daily basis. You haven't been taking care of business. You've been falling behind."

"Gee, what's going to happen?" asked Brother as the living room phone rang.

"It's the BRS," said
Mama. "For you, Papa."

"Take their number
and I'll call them back,"
said Papa.

"What's the BRS,
Mama?" asked Sister.

"It's the Bears'
Revenue Service," said
Mama. "They collect
taxes."

"What's going to happen,"
said Papa, "is that there's
not going to be any more
Mars space station. No
more boom box. No more
popcorn. It's just you and
your homework until you're
all caught up."